S0-BOL-568

Also by Raymond Briggs:

The Elephant and the Bad Baby
Father Christmas (Goes on Holiday)
Fungus the Bogeyman
The Snowman
Gentleman Jim
When the Wind Blows
The Fungus the Bogeyman Plop-up Book

*

The Mother Goose Treasury

The Fairy Tale Treasury
(with Virginia Haviland)

FATHER CHRISTMAS

RAYMOND BRIGGS

Father Christmas

HAMISH HAMILTON
London

For my Mother and Father

© 1973 Raymond Briggs
All rights reserved
First published in Great Britain 1973 by
Hamish Hamilton Children's Books
Garden House, 57-59 Long Acre, London WC2E 9JZ
Reprinted 1973, 1974, 1976, 1977, 1978, 1980, 1982, 1983
ISBN 0 241 02260 6
Printed and bound in Spain by Grijelmo, Bilbao

Father Christmas

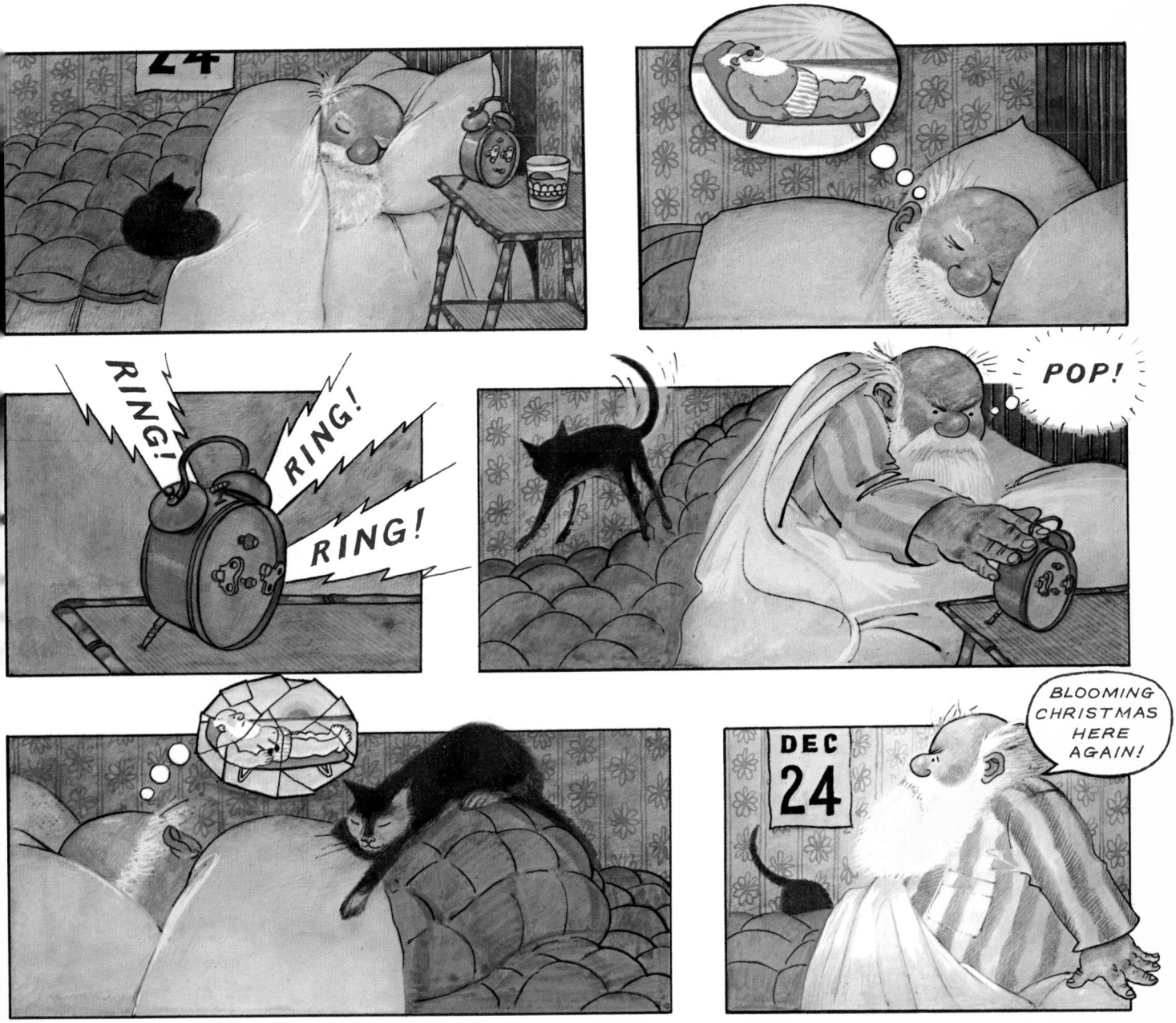

GET OFF MY SLIPPERS, DOG!

BLOOMING SNOW!
MAJORCA

YAWN

I HATE WINTER!

HERE YOU ARE, DEERS.

GOOD
OT OF
TEA
TEA
BLOW THE BLOOMING SNOW!
THE FROZEN NORTH WILL BE VERY COLD - SNOW, ICE, SLEET....
BRRR!
GOOD GIRL!

CAPRI
CORN FLAKES
ROLL ON SUMMER!
ARCTIC ECHO
SNOW, SNOW AND MORE SNOW
MALTA
MANGO CHUTNEY
UXO
UXO
BRR! BLOOMING COLD!
WORK, WORK, WORK!

KEEP STILL YOU SILLY DEERS !

TEA

GOODBYE CAT
GOODBYE DOG

GIDDY UP!
TALLY-HO!

BLOOMING SNOW!
RAIN NOW! WHAT NEXT?

!!! xxx
WEATHER!
FOG!

BLOOMING CHIMNEYS!

BLOOMING SOOT !
THIS WAY PLEASE

BRIGHTON
LANE
UNDERHILL
DITCHLING
CATTLE

HM, BETTER THAN NOTHING I SUPPOSE.
FOR FATHER CHRISTMAS

WHOA!

63
65
67

TEA
TEA

SNOW, ICE, FROST, SLEET, HAIL, RAIN
GRRR!

BLOOMING AERIALS!
FOR FATHER CHRISTMAS
BLOOMING CATS!
BETTER GET A MOVE ON!
HM, NO BLOOMING CHIMNEYS, ANYWAY.
DAFT PLACE TO LIVE!

BLOOMING COOKERS!
STAIRS, STAIRS, STAIRS.
DEAR SANTA DAD SAYS HELP YOURSELF
LOVELY!
HOW DO I GET INTO THIS THING?
AAACHOO!
GETTING A BLOOMING COLD, NOW.
MILK
ERB 1900
STILL AT IT, MATE?
NEARLY DONE.
ONLY ONE MORE, NOW.

GOOD! THE FLAG'S FLYING. THEY'RE IN.

WHOA!
HOORAY! HOME AGAIN.

BRR! BLOOMING FEET FROZEN!

HULLO, CAT! HULLO, DOG!

NICE CLEAN STRAW, DEERS.

GOOD CUP OF TEA.

TEA

TEA
♫ HARK THE HERALD ANGELS SING ♫

LOVELY PUD!

HM! PRESENTS! SEEN ENOUGH OF THOSE THINGS FOR ONE DAY.

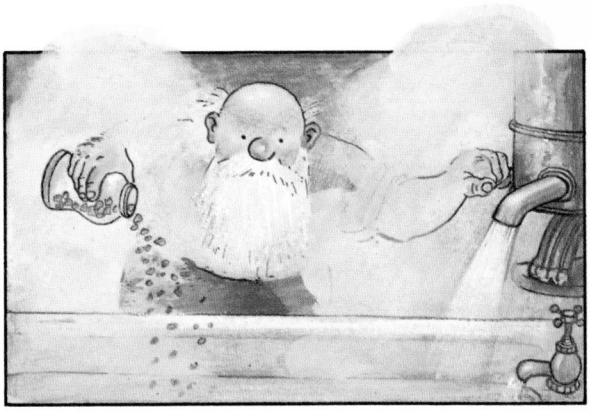

NOTHING LIKE A GOOD BATH.

♫ HARK THE HERALD ANGELS SING ♫

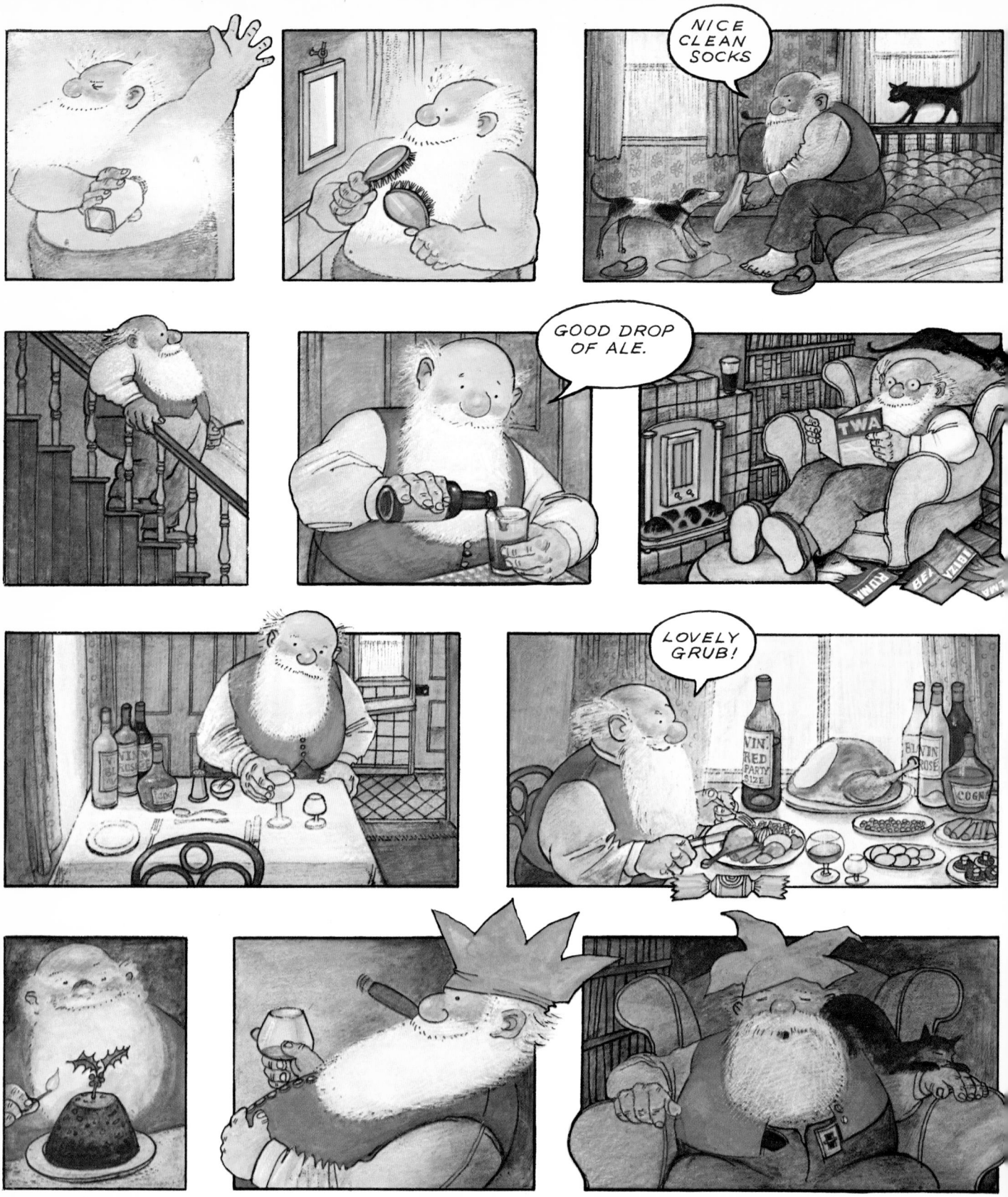
NICE CLEAN SOCKS
GOOD DROP OF ALE.
LOVELY GRUB!
VIN. RED PARTY SIZE
COGN

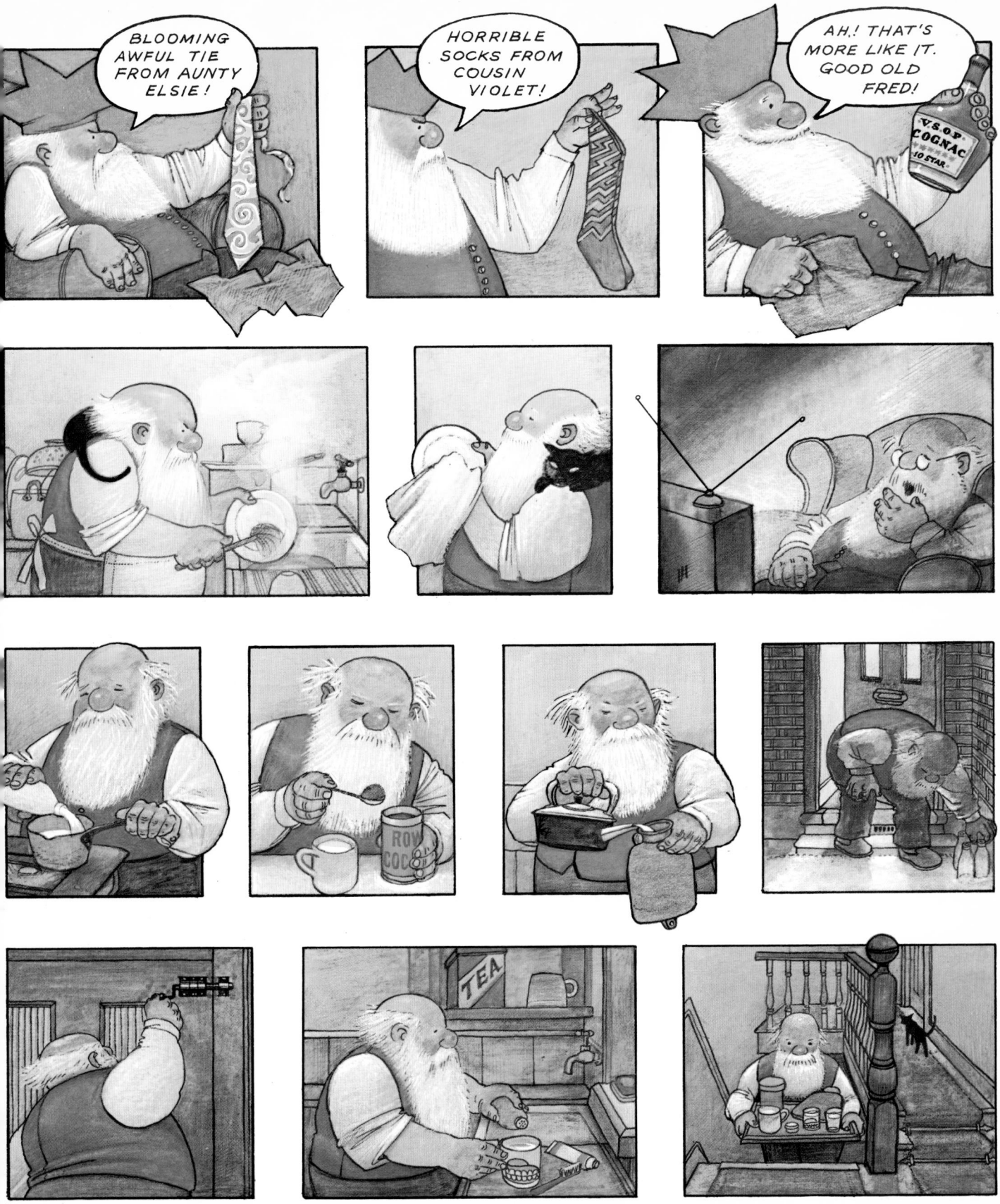
BLOOMING AWFUL TIE FROM AUNTY ELSIE!
HORRIBLE SOCKS FROM COUSIN VIOLET!
AH,! THAT'S MORE LIKE IT. GOOD OLD FRED!
V.S.O.P. COGNAC 10 STAR
TEA

FIDDLING BUTTONS!
DEC 24
DEC 25
THAT'S THAT DONE FOR ANOTHER YEAR.
HAPPY CHRISTMAS CAT!
HAPPY CHRISTMAS DOG!
HAPPY BLOOMING CHRISTMAS TO YOU, TOO!

The End